D1139391

Usborne
Classic Stories
for Little
Children

Contents

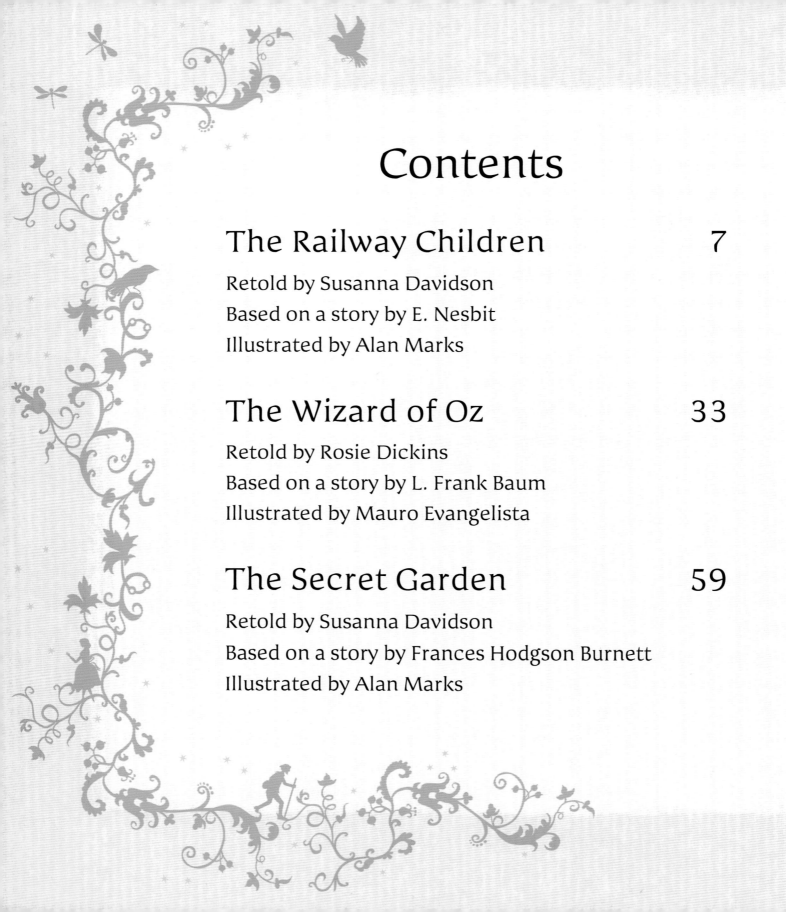

The Railway Children   7

Retold by Susanna Davidson
Based on a story by E. Nesbit
Illustrated by Alan Marks

The Wizard of Oz   33

Retold by Rosie Dickins
Based on a story by L. Frank Baum
Illustrated by Mauro Evangelista

The Secret Garden   59

Retold by Susanna Davidson
Based on a story by Frances Hodgson Burnett
Illustrated by Alan Marks

The Wind in the Willows 83

Retold by Lesley Sims

Based on a story by Kenneth Grahame

Illustrated by Mauro Evangelista

The Story of Heidi 109

Retold by Susanna Davidson

Based on a story by Johanna Spyri

Illustrated by Alan Marks

The Railway Children

Bobbie, Peter and Phyllis had everything they wanted —
pretty clothes, heaps of toys and a loving mother and father.

Then, on Peter's eighth birthday,
the trouble began.

After the birthday tea, the doorbell rang, sharply.
Three men came in and took Father away with them.

"Where's he gone?" asked Peter.
"He hasn't packed any clothes."

"He had to go quickly — on business,"
said Mother, her eyes bright with tears.

After that,
everything changed.

All the furniture was sold.
The servants left.
Mother was hardly ever at home.

"We have to play at being poor for a while," she said. "We're going to live in the countryside."

They arrived at the new house, late at night. "Let's explore tomorrow," said Peter.

Early the next morning they raced outside, through the garden, down the hill, until they came to a railway track.

There was a great rumbling sound and with a WHOOSH, a train shot out of the tunnel.

It's like a dragon!

"Perhaps it's going to London," yelled Phyllis, above the noise.

"Maybe that's where Father is," said Bobbie.
"If it's a magic train, it'll take our love to him. Let's wave."

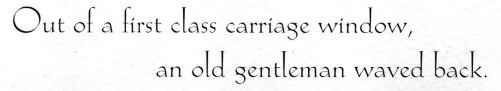

Out of a first class carriage window,
an old gentleman waved back.

Every day after that, the children ran down to
the railway to wave to the old gentleman,
and to send their love to Father.

"Let's do something different," Peter suggested one day.
"We could walk along the path by the track."

But when they reached the path,
they heard a strange rumbling noise.

The trees on the bank started sliding downhill,
then fell onto the railway track
with a deafening roar.

"Oh!" cried Peter. "The 11:29 train will
be along any minute. There'll be a terrible
accident. We must do something."

17

"Our red petticoats!" Bobbie exclaimed. "Red is for danger! Let's tear them up and use them as flags."

The train thundered closer. The others sprang out of the way, but Bobbie didn't move. She knew it was dangerous, but she had to make it stop.

With a squeal of brakes the train shuddered to a halt.
"What's going on?" cried the driver.
Peter pointed to the landslide.

The driver gasped in shock. "You children saved lives today," he said.

The Railway Company held a celebration for the children to thank them, with a brass band, bunting and cake.

The Railway Director gave them each a gold watch,
but best of all, their own old gentleman was there.

"Do come back for tea," said Phyllis.

At home, Bobbie took the old gentleman's coat.
She glanced at his newspaper, then stopped and stared.
There was a photograph of Father.

"SPY TRIAL!"
it said.
Then:
"GUILTY"
and
"FIVE YEARS
IN JAIL."

"Oh Daddy!" she cried. "You didn't do it."
Bobbie ran to her room to hide her tears.

"Mother didn't want us to know," she realized.
"She didn't want to worry us."

After tea, when the old gentleman
had gone, Mother came to find
her. Bobbie cried and cried,
but wouldn't say why.

Bobbie was desperate to help.
She decided to write a letter
to the old gentleman.

Dear Friend,

See what it says in this paper.

That is our Father, but he isn't a spy.

Could you find out who did it,

and then they would let Father out of prison.

Just think if it was your Daddy,

how would you feel? Please help me.

Love from,

Bobbie

Time passed, and nothing happened.
Bobbie missed Father so badly,
her mind was filled with wanting him.

Then, one late summer's day,
Bobbie found herself walking to the station, as if in a dream.

She arrived just as a train pulled into the platform.
Only three people got out. An old woman,
the grocer's wife and the third...

"Oh! My Daddy,
my Daddy!"
Bobbie's cry pierced
the air.

"I can't believe you're really here," said Bobbie,
as they walked up the hill together.

"Didn't Mother get my letter?" Father asked.
"They found the real spy. Your old friend helped catch him."

"Now run ahead," he said, "and tell everyone I'm back."

He came up the garden path,
his heart beating fast.
Mother, Bobbie, Peter and Phyllis
stood in the doorway.

"You're home!" they cried.
"You're home at last."

With his arms out wide to hug them all,
Father went into the house.
We won't follow him. In this happy moment,
it's time for us to say goodbye.

The Wizard of Oz

Dorothy lived on a lonely farm
with her uncle and aunt
and her little dog, Toto.

WOOF!

One day, the wind began to howl.
"It's a whirlwind!" cried Dorothy's aunt.
"Everyone to the cellar!"

But Toto had dashed for
cover under the bed.

The wind blew harder...

and harder...

until suddenly...

it spun the house into the air.

The house sailed through the sky...
and landed with a **BUMP!**

Dorothy poked her head outside
and saw some friendly faces.

"Welcome to Oz!"

"Please, how do I get home?" she asked.

"You'll need to see the wizard," said a woman. "He lives in Emerald City, at the end of the yellow brick road."

And she gave Dorothy a pair of sparkling silver shoes for the journey.

Dorothy's new shoes tinkled on the yellow
bricks, as she walked along the road.

"Hello there!" called a scarecrow.
"Where are you going?"

"To see the wizard," replied Dorothy.

"Can I come with you?" said the
scarecrow. "I want to ask the
wizard for some brains."

"Of course," said Dorothy,
with a smile.

A few miles on, they saw a tinman. He stood stock still, his arms stuck behind his head. "Help!" he grunted. "I've rusted up."

Dorothy picked up a nearby oilcan and trickled oil onto his stiff joints. "We're on our way to see the wizard," she said.

"Can I come?" asked the tinman. "I want to ask the wizard for a heart."

They had barely set off again, when a lion leaped out of the trees with a terrible **ROAR!**

The scarecrow trembled but Toto barked.

"Oh!" yelped the lion. "Don't hurt me."

"I heard you talking about the wizard and I want him to make me brave. Let me come with you."

The four of them followed the yellow
brick road as it wound on and on,
past forests and rivers and fields.

At last, they came to a city of glittering emeralds.

A gatekeeper gave them each a pair of green glasses and led them to the wizard's palace.

But the wizard wouldn't help them for nothing.

"First, you must kill the wicked witch!" he demanded.

The wicked witch lived in a castle guarded by wolves and crows.

Grrrrr

But the tinman fought
off the wolves.

And the scarecrow scared away the crows.

Furious, the witch summoned her flying monkeys.
Soon the friends were prisoners in her castle.

"Now you're my slaves," she cackled.

"Get to work!"

Then the witch noticed Dorothy's beautiful silver shoes.

"I want those shoes," thought the witch.

She waited until
Dorothy was fetching
a pail of water...

...then she
pushed her
and pounced.

Dorothy was so annoyed, she threw the water
all over the witch, drenching her.

At once, the
witch melted away
into a puddle.

"She's gone!" cried Dorothy,
quickly putting on her shoes.
"We can claim our rewards."

The wizard's rewards were rather strange.

First, he gave
the scarecrow a
handful of pins.

"Now I'm as sharp as a pin."

Then he gave
the tinman a
heart-shaped
cushion.

And for the lion, there was
a bottle marked **Courage**.

Last of all, the wizard showed
Dorothy a hot-air balloon.
"We'll fly home!" he said.

But the ropes snapped and the balloon took off without her.
"Go to the good witch Glinda!" called the wizard. "She'll help you."

Dorothy was in despair, but her friends took her to Glinda's palace.

"I'm stuck in Oz!" Dorothy sobbed,
standing before the throne.

"Don't worry," said Glinda, kindly.
"The silver shoes will take you home."

"Just knock the heels
together and wish."

55

Dorothy whirled through the air...

When she landed, she was back on her aunt and uncle's farm.
She raced to her aunt and threw her arms around her.

"I've been on an amazing adventure," Dorothy told her.
"But oh! I'm so glad to be home."

And Toto barked as if to say, "Me too!"

The Secret Garden

The last time Mary Lennox saw her parents
was in the garden outside their house, in India.

That night, a terrible fever swept through the house.
Mary's mother and father both died.

Mary felt as if she were all
alone in the world.

Then a letter arrived from her
uncle, Mr. Craven,
inviting her to England to stay.

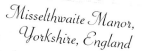

Misselthwaite Manor,
Yorkshire, England

Dear Mary,

I have made arrangements for you to come
to England and live at Misselthwaite Manor.
My housekeeper will meet you in London
and escort you here.

I'm afraid I won't see you for some time as
I have to travel to Europe on business.

Yours sincerely,

Archibald Craven

"I don't like it here," thought Mary,
as she crossed the wild, windswept moors.

She arrived at the house late at night.

Her uncle was away, the housekeeper said,
and left her alone in a shadowy room.

Outside, the wind howled like a lonely person.

In the morning, Mary wandered out of the house into a wintry garden, where an old man was digging.

"What's behind that wall?" she asked.

"Ah," said the gardener.
"That's the secret garden. Mr. Craven shut it up when his wife died. Then he buried the key and went away."

As he spoke, a robin fluttered up and perched nearby.

He cocked his head and looked at Mary.
"Will you be friends with me?" she whispered.

"You sound just like our Dickon," said the gardener.

"He talks to all wild things.
Now run along, missy. I've got work to do."

Mary watched the robin fly off and decided to follow him.
"Show me the key to the garden," she begged.

The robin swooped down, and hopped around on the ground.

"He *is* trying to show me something,"
thought Mary.

She scrabbled in the soil
and found... a rusty key.

Mary searched and
searched for the
door to the
garden.

Then, one day, when the wind came
in sweet-scented gusts from the moor, she found it.

She put the key in the lock
and the door creaked slowly open...

Mary was inside
the secret garden.

It was a magical, mysterious place.

A hazy tangle of rose branches and
spiky green shoots thrust up
through the wintry ground.

Mary spent all morning in the garden, entranced.

The shoots looked so crowded, she cleared spaces around them.

The robin chirped, as though pleased someone
was gardening here at last.

Outside, she saw a boy with a fawn by his side.

"Are you Dickon?" she asked shyly.
He nodded.

"Can you keep a secret?"
Mary asked.

"I keep secrets all the time," Dickon replied. "Secrets about fox cubs and birds' nests. Aye, I can keep a secret."

"Come with me," whispered Mary,
and led him to the secret garden.
Dickon looked around as if in a dream.

"I never thought I'd see this place," he murmured.
"Help me make it come alive," said Mary.

"Yes," whispered Dickon.
"We'll make it the prettiest garden in England."

The winter passed into spring.
One blustery night, Mary couldn't
sleep. She was woken by a cry
that pierced the wind.

She followed it
down dark passages,
until she reached a door
with a glimmer of light beneath.

Inside the room was a vast carved bed
with a boy in the middle of it, sobbing.

"Are you a ghost?" whispered Mary.

"No!" he snapped. "I'm Colin Craven."

"Mr. Craven's my uncle," said Mary.
"Are we cousins? Why did no one tell me about you?"

"I'm not well," Colin replied. "My mother died when
I was born and my father can't bear to look at me."

"Just like the secret garden," said Mary.

And she told him all about it...
the sun and rain and buds bursting into flower,

while Colin closed his eyes
and dreamed of a garden, coming alive.

74

Mary rushed to Colin's room the next morning.

"I've brought a friend to meet you," she said.

"Will you take me to the garden?" asked Colin.

They rushed down the paths. Mary flung back the ivy and opened the garden door.

Sunshine lit up sprays of flowers
and the air was alive with birdsong.

"I can feel things growing," gasped Colin.

"You can work with us in the garden," said Mary.

Colin's pale face grew rosy in the sunlight.
"And maybe I'll get well," he whispered.

Every day they played and worked in the garden
and, every day, Colin grew stronger.

"If only my father could see me," thought Colin.

And he began to wish,

"Come home, come home."

One night, Colin's father, far away in Italy,
had a strange dream. He heard his dead wife calling his name.

"Where are you?" he pleaded.

"In the garden,"
came the reply.

Mr. Craven returned home at once. He rushed to the garden.

As he came down the path,
    he heard children laughing behind the wall.

"How can that be?" he thought.
"The garden must be dead...
I buried the key."

At that moment, Colin and Mary burst out of the garden door.

"Colin?" gasped his father. "Is that really you?"

"I'm better, Father. I'm well at last.
It was Mary, and the garden."

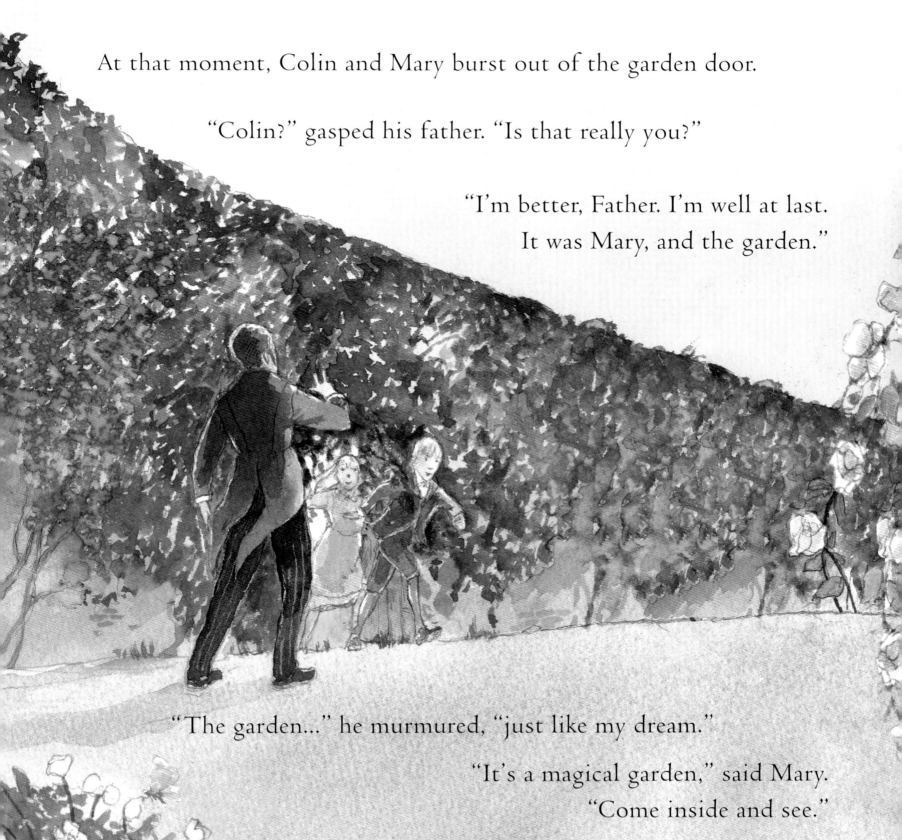

"The garden..." he murmured, "just like my dream."

"It's a magical garden," said Mary.
"Come inside and see."

The Wind in the Willows

Ratty and Mole were out for a row,
just messing about on the river.

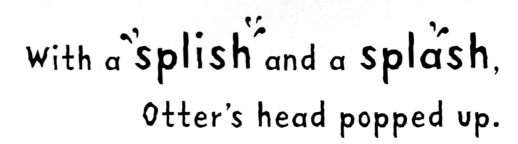

with a "splish" and a "splash,"
Otter's head popped up.

"Hello you two!" he gurgled.
"Toad is looking for you."

Toad Hall stood grand and tall, right on the edge of the river.

Ratty rowed there at once.

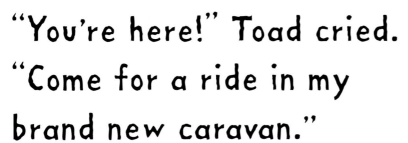

"You're here!" Toad cried. "Come for a ride in my brand new caravan."

They rambled along the country lanes, talking of this and of that.

Insects were humming and birds were chirping, when...

Poop! Poop!

A sports car shot past in a cloud of smoke, sending everyone flying.

"Scoundrels!" shouted Ratty.

"Villains!" muttered Mole.

"Poop! Poop!" said Toad. "Forget that boring old caravan. I'm buying a car."

From that moment, Toad was hooked.
Cars were all he could think about.

He drove them, he dreamed about
them and he cheered when
he saw a new one.

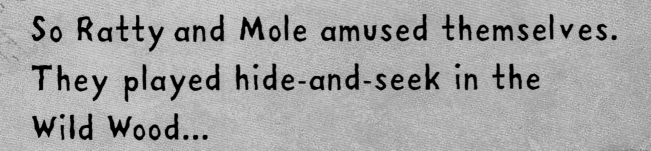

So Ratty and Mole amused themselves.
They played hide-and-seek in the
Wild Wood...

...or stayed with
their friend, Badger.

91

"How's Toad?" asked Badger one night, over cookies and cocoa. "Still buying new cars?"

"Buying them and crashing them," said Ratty. "He's the World's Worst Driver."

"We'll have to help him," Badger declared. "Tomorrow, we'll pay him a visit..."

"Hello you fellows!" said Toad, early the next morning. "I'm just off for a drive."

"Oh no you're not," said Badger.
"You're a menace on the road.
We're taking your keys and
keeping you inside."

"It's for your own
good Toad," added Mole.

"They won't stop me!" Toad chuckled, as he escaped. "I'll find a car to drive."

Soon he saw the
perfect one.
As if in a dream,
he clambered in...
...and sped away.

That night, Toad was in prison.
"Oh, why did I steal a car?"
he thought.

"Oh clever Badger, oh sensible Mole,
oh
foolish,
foolish
Toad."

Toad was down – but not for long.

Late one night, he escaped
from prison, cunningly
disguised as a
washerwoman.

When the moon was high in the sky,
he curled up by a tree and
snuggled into his shawl.

He fell asleep, dreaming of home.

But back at Toad Hall – calamity! His home had been stolen from him by stealthy stoats and wicked weasels.

"Don't panic, Toad," said Mole.
"Badger has a plan."

And Badger did, for he knew of a secret
tunnel that would take them right
into Toad Hall.

In the dead of night, armed with sticks and swords, they followed Badger down the secret tunnel...

...and burst out into the kitchen.

"CHARGE!" hollered Badger.

What a squealing and a screeching
filled the air.
"Take my house would you? Take that!"
shouted Toad.

WHAM!

The stoats and the weasels were
banished forever. Toad was so thrilled,
he held a small party to celebrate.

And he never drove another car again.

The Story of Heidi

The wind whistled and sang.
 It blew in great gusts at Heidi and her aunt,
  as they battled their way up the mountain.

Up and up they went,
 to a world above the clouds.

At last they came to a small hut,
perched on the top
of the mountain.

A fierce old man opened the door.

111

"Meet your granddaughter!" said Heidi's aunt.
"I've brought her to live with you."

But I don't want her!

"I've looked after Heidi since her parents died. Now it's your turn," her aunt declared.

And with that she ran
back down the mountain.

"Well, you'd better come in,"
said Grandfather, gruffly.

"You'll have to find your
own place to sleep though."

"What's up the ladder?"
asked Heidi.

Grandfather didn't reply.

Heidi climbed into a hayloft.

There, she made
a sweet-smelling
bed out of hay.

The next morning,
Heidi woke to the
sound of bells.

Sunlight poured in
through the window.

She ran outside onto the dewy wet grass,
where a boy was whistling.

"This is Peter, the goat boy," said Grandfather.

"Do you want to come up the mountain with me?"
Peter asked. "I'm taking the goats to find fresh grass."

Heidi went out with Peter and the goats every day.

In the evenings, Grandfather
fed her creamy goat's milk,
crusty bread and melted cheese.

"Read me a story," pleaded Heidi.

So, every night, Grandfather read her
a story by the fire.

Heidi had never been happier...
until one morning, her aunt came back.

"I've found a job for Heidi," she announced.
"I'm taking her to town."

"Poor Grandfather," cried Heidi.
"He'll be all alone."

"He likes it that way," said her aunt.

"He doesn't!" thought
Heidi. "One day I'll
come back to him."

Heidi's aunt took her
to a grand house.

There, she had to
look after a sick
little girl, called Clara.

"I'm so weak I can
hardly walk," said Clara.
"You'd soon get well
in the mountains,"
Heidi replied.

The town was full of jostling people.
Stale smells filled the streets.

NO
DOGS

NO
BALL
GAMES

Heidi longed for her hayloft,
for the jingling bells of the goats,
for stories by the fire...

At night, Heidi sleepwalked.
She wandered the house
in her white nightgown.

"That girl needs to go home,"
Clara's father decided.

A week later, Grandfather saw a strange procession coming up the mountain.

Heidi! You've come back to me.

"Clara wanted to come too,"
Heidi explained.

"Can she stay until she's well again?"

"Of course," said Grandfather.
"We'll help her get better."

Clara drank fresh
goat's milk every
morning, and
sat outside in
the sunshine.

And every day,
she walked
a little more.

"I can't believe it," said Clara's father,
when he came for her.

"Is this really my daughter?
How can I ever thank you?"

Clara... walking!

When Clara and her father had gone,
Heidi and Grandfather went outside
to watch the sunset.

"You're home now," said Grandfather.
"I'll never let you go again."

About the Authors

E. Nesbit 1858-1924

Edith Nesbit was born in Kennington, London but her father died when she was still a young child, and the family moved around a lot. When she was 19, she met Hubert Bland and they married three years later.

Edith and Hubert were very interested in politics and helped to found a group named the Fabian Society, which called for more fairness in the world. At the same time, Edith was writing children's books. During her lifetime, she wrote over 40 books for children, including *The Story of the Treasure Seekers*, *The Wouldbegoods*, *Five Children and It*, *The Phoenix and the Carpet* and *The Enchanted Castle*. Many of these have since been made into films and television series.

L. Frank Baum 1856-1919

L. Frank Baum grew up in a wealthy American family.
He had several jobs before becoming a writer, including running
a store and breeding chickens. *The Wizard of Oz* was an instant hit when
it was published, sparking off a whole series of books
set in Oz, as well as a famous film.

Frances Hodgson Burnett 1849-1924

Frances Hodgson Burnett was born in Manchester, England.
After her father's death, the family moved to Tennessee,
America in 1865, where they struggled to earn a living. At 17,
Frances sold her first story. She went on to write many novels. Her
other children's books include *A Little Princess* and
Little Lord Fauntleroy.

Kenneth Grahame 1859-1932

When he was a young boy, Kenneth Grahame loved playing in his grandmother's garden by a river. As an adult, he worked for the Bank of England, but he wrote in his spare time. He never forgot the fun days he had spent down by the river, and he immortalized them in his novel *The Wind in the Willows*. The book was written for his son, Alastair, and first published in 1908.

Johanna Spyri 1827-1901

Johanna Spyri, a doctor's daughter, was born
in the Swiss countryside. She grew up loving the
mountains. *The Story of Heidi* was first published
over a hundred years ago, in 1881, and is still
a much-loved children's book today.

The Railway Children, *The Secret Garden* and *The Story of Heidi*
are based on adaptations by Mary Sebag-Montefiore

Additional illustration by Candice Whatmore

Designed by Katarina Dragoslavic, Louise Flutter,
Hannah Ahmed and Anna Gould

Cover design by Russell Punter

Edited by Jenny Tyler

Digital manipulation by John Russell

First published in 2009 by Usborne Publishing Ltd, 83-85 Saffron Hill, London EC1N 8RT, England.
www.usborne.com Copyright © 2009, Usborne Publishing Ltd. The name Usborne and the devices ♀ ⊕ are Trade Marks
of Usborne Publishing Ltd. All rights reserved. No part of this publication may be reproduced, stored in a retrieval system,
or transmitted in any form or by any means, electronic, mechanical, photocopying, recording or otherwise,
without the prior permission of the publisher. First published in America in 2009. UE.